T0288473

Around the World

CONTENTS

NATIONAL GEOGRAPHIC School Publishing
Hampton-Brown

Words with oo, ue

Look at each picture. Read the words.

Example:

bl**ue**

igl**oo**

m**oo**n

racc**oo**n

gl**ue**

bl**ue**jeans

High Frequency Words
above
better
far
full
goes
long
something
talk
watch
while

Key Words

This Friday, Oona gets to stay up late with her mom! Read the list of things they plan to do. Match each thing to a picture.

Fun Night with Mom!

1. We'll **watch** TV **while** the baby **goes** to sleep.
2. While he sleeps **above** us, we'll **talk** to Grandma on the phone for a **long** time.
3. We'll read about places **far** away.
4. We'll make **something** good to eat—nuts are good but popcorn is **better**—and eat until we are **full**!

What is something you would add to the list?

Phonics Games
NGReach.com

While You Sleep

by Kelsey Bruce

Fran sleeps.

While you sleep, many things happen on Earth. Some things take place at night. Others happen in daylight. Why?

Ming goes to class.

If it's midnight where you are, it's noon on the other side of Earth. It's true! Fran snoozes in Bloomfield, while Ming goes to class in China.

It is a hot, sunny day for Ming. At the same time, it is a cold, gloomy night for Fran. Why does this happen?

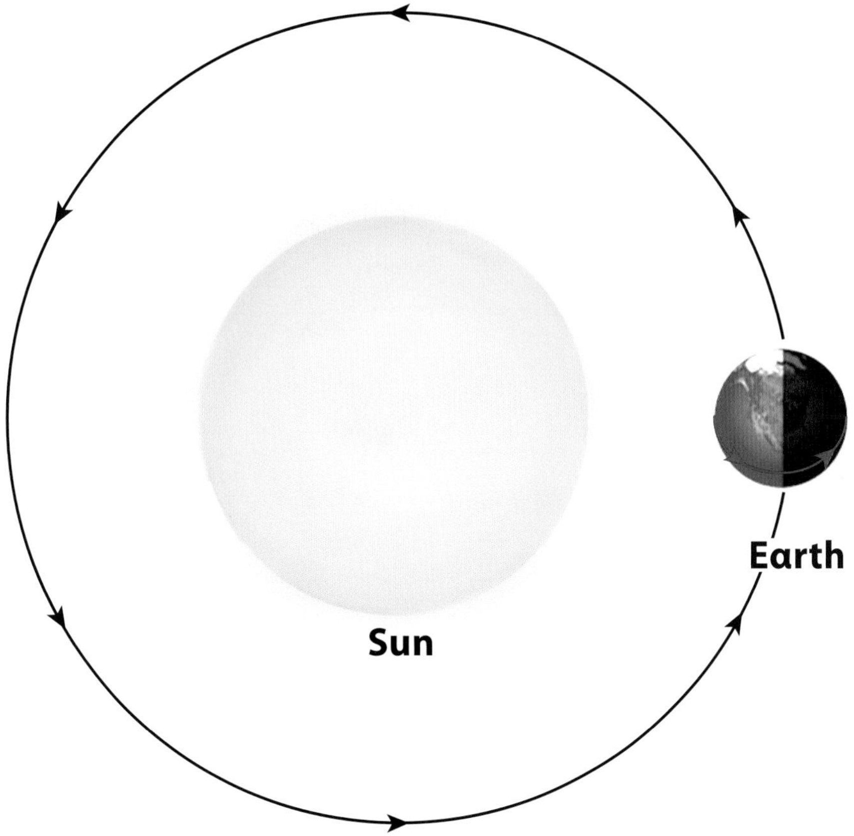

It is due to the fact that Earth spins all the time. The part facing the Sun gets light. As Earth spins, it looks like the Sun is traveling through the sky. But it is Earth that is moving!

bird

skunk

Let's talk about the things that happen at night. As you go to sleep, many animals wake up. These animals like night better than day.

bat

lynx

Many of these animals hunt for food at night. Birds and bats swoop down to grab a meal. Big cats sit silently. They wait for clueless animals to pass by. Then they grab them!

wolf

fox

Animals in hot places wait for the coolness of night to leave their homes. They scoot around in the moonlight to find food.

mice

raccoon

Some sneaky animals wait for night to snoop around our homes for something they want to eat. Raccoons, mice, and rats all seem to know when we are sleeping!

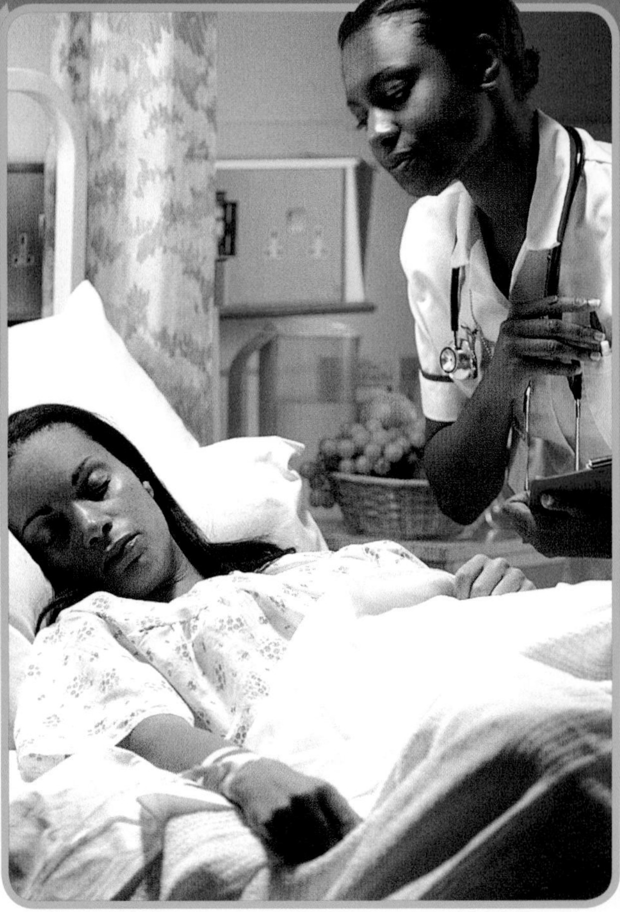

While you sleep, some people are hard at work. They might be making things that we need. They might be helping the sick.

People work at night to keep us safe, too. They keep watch through the long night. Each is a true hero when we need help!

The moon works at night, too! It helps move the tides. And when the moon is full, it lights up the sky. But the moon seems to change shape every night. We see less and less of it until it's black. Then we see more and more. Check the sky above for proof! ❖

Words with **oo, ue**

Read these words.

baby	balloon	blue	child	stool
lady	man	scoop	shampoo	cool

Find the words with **oo** or **ue**.
Use letters to build them.

b l u e

Talk Together

Ricky Raccoon has a bad habit. He looks in people's rooms at night! Choose words from the box above to tell your partner what Ricky Raccoon sees in the rooms tonight.

He sees a child
getting a blue stool.

Endings -er, -est

Look at each picture. Read the words.

bigg**est** tini**er** tini**est**

low**est** high**er** high**est**

slow**est** fast**er** fast**est**

High Frequency Words
above
better
far
full
goes
long
something
talk
watch
while

Key Words

Dad is on a work trip. Read the note he wrote to his son, Zeke. Look at the picture of the place he writes about.

May 5

Dear Zeke,

There is a **full** moon **above** me tonight. I'll take a **long** run on the beach. It's **better** running on sand than on a road. I can **watch** as the tide **goes** out. I wish you weren't so **far** away! You could run with me. We'd **talk** **while** we run. Then we'd get **something** to eat. Say hi to Mom. I'll be home soon!

I miss you,

Dad

What would you like to do at a beach?

GO! Phonics Games

NGReach.com

The Ocean Tides

by Donovan Brock

Oceans make up about 3/4 of Earth. The level of these seas changes every day.

Tides MAY, 2010 — TEXAS CITY, TX					
Day	**High/Low Tides**	**Time**	**Height (in feet)**	**Time**	**Height (in feet)**
Sat. May 22	High tide	12:45 AM	1.1	1:10 PM	1.3
	Low tide	6:41 AM	0.7	7:06 PM	0.4
Sun. May 23	High tide	1:35 AM	1.3	2:00 PM	1.3
	Low tide	7:31 AM	1.0	7:56 PM	0.1
Mon. May 24	High tide	2:25 AM	1.5	2:50 PM	1.3
	Low tide	8:21 AM	1.1	8:46 PM	0.2
Tue. May 25	High tide	3:15 AM	1.7	3:40 PM	1.3
	Low tide	9:11 AM	1.2	9:36 PM	0.3

Sea level goes from highest to lowest twice each day. This rise and fall of water is the ocean tides.

Watch the tides go in and out on the beach. See where the water stops on the sand. In a while, see if it stops nearer to the ocean or above the line on the sand.

If the water stops closer to the ocean, it is going to low tide. If it stops higher on the beach, it is going to high tide.

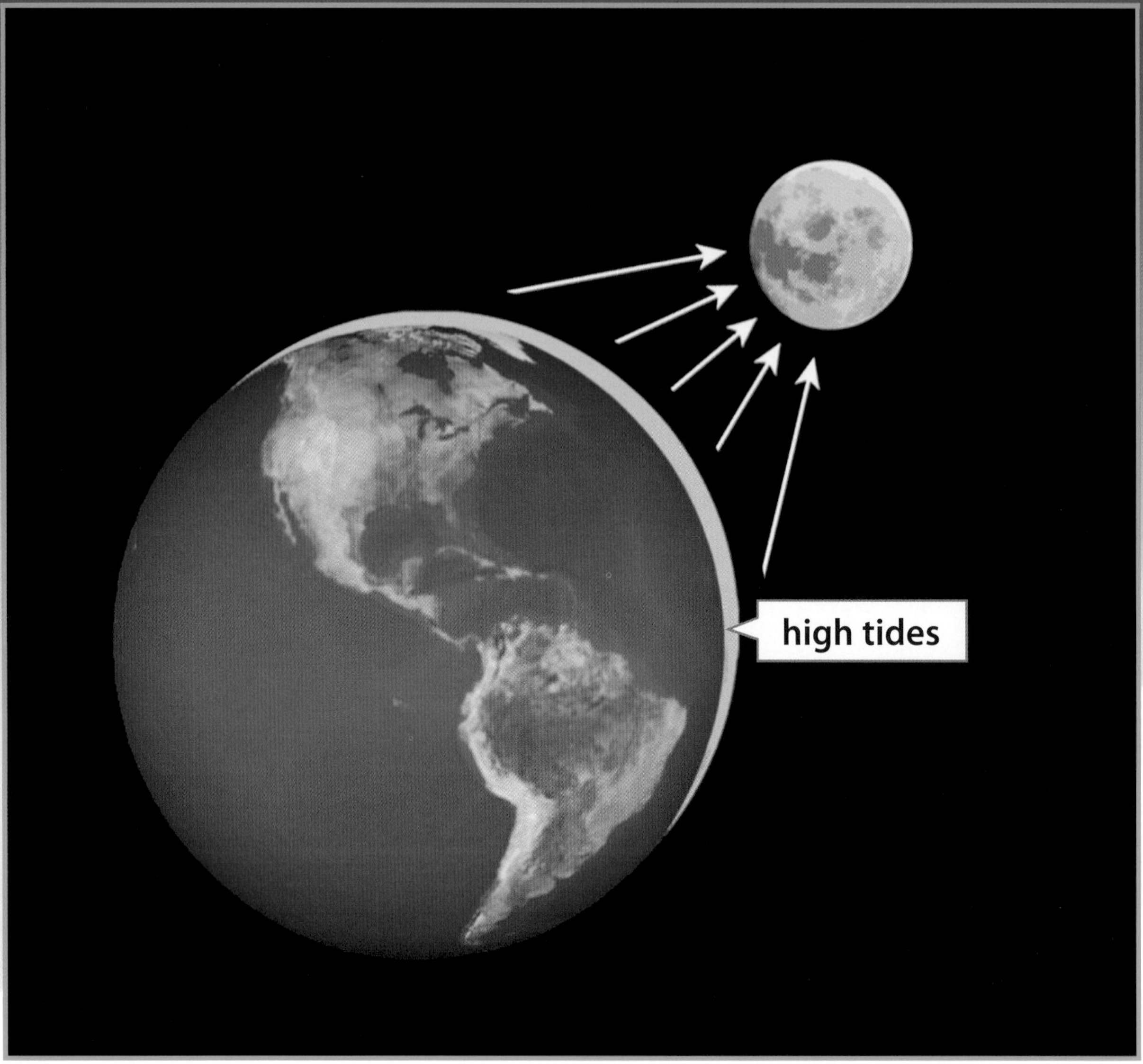

Why are there tides? A force called gravity makes the moon tug at the water on Earth. This tug is strongest for the oceans closest to the moon. That's high tide!

The other side of Earth, the part farthest from the moon, gets low tide. But the moon moves around Earth. Bit by bit, the tug gets stronger where it was low tide. Bit by bit, low tide grows to be high tide.

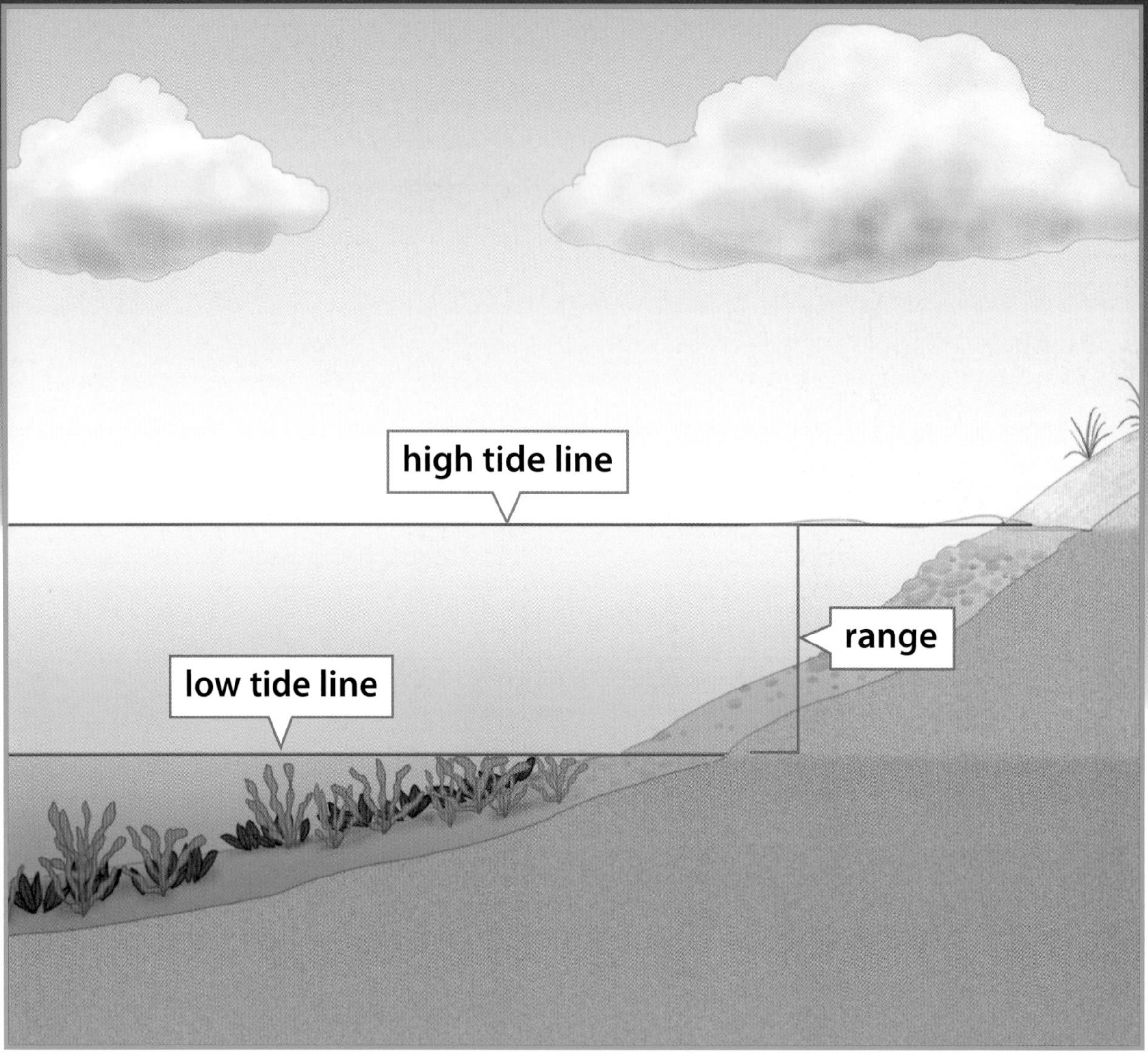

The water level changes as it goes from high to low tide. This change is called its range.

The ocean range at the Bay of Fundy is about 40 feet!

The range in the ocean is 2 to 3 feet. The range is bigger at the coast. It may be 6 to 10 feet. In big lakes, the range is much slighter. It may be less than 2 inches!

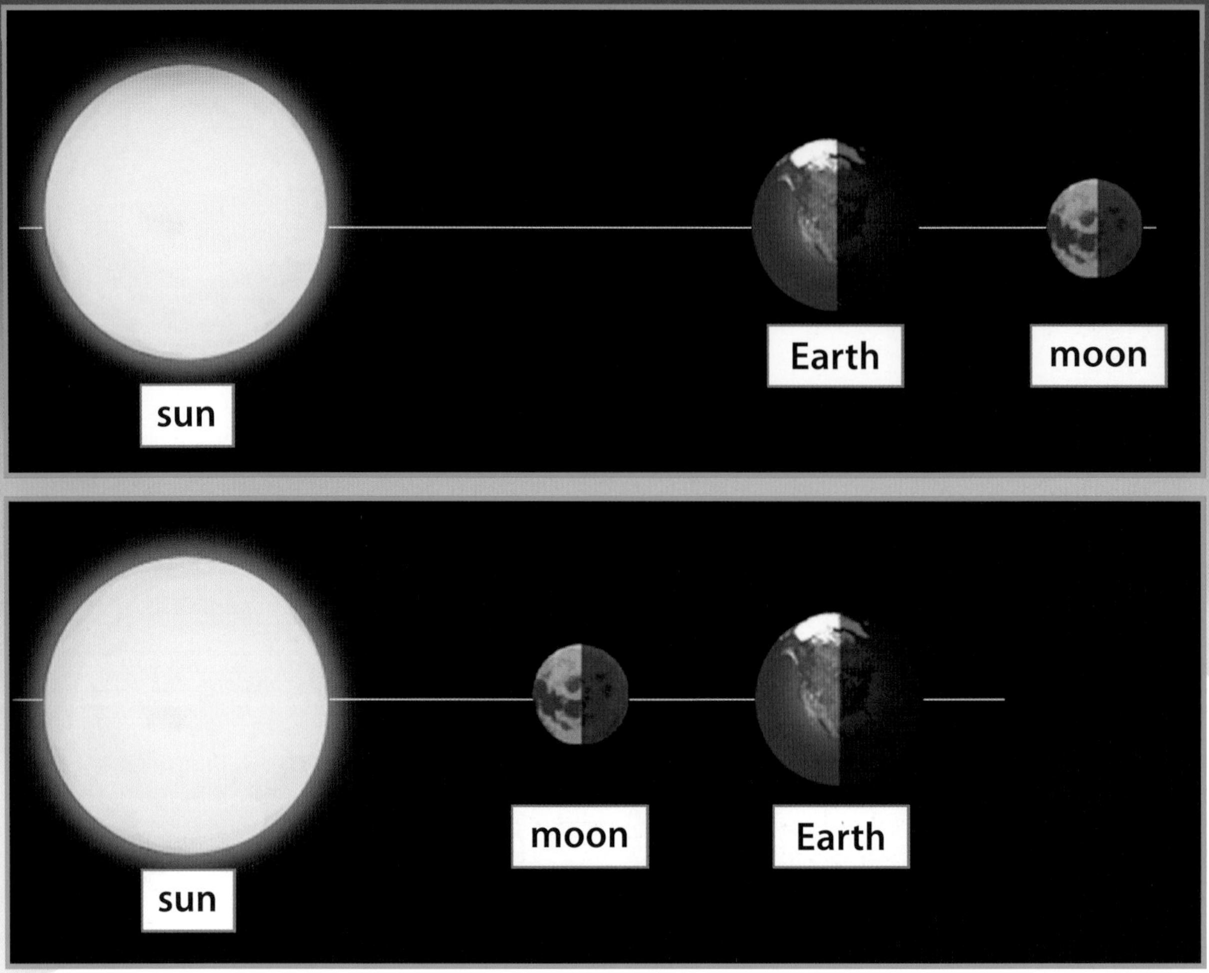

The range of tides in one place changes, too. This is due to how the Earth, moon, and sun line up. Every 2 weeks or so, all 3 are in a line.

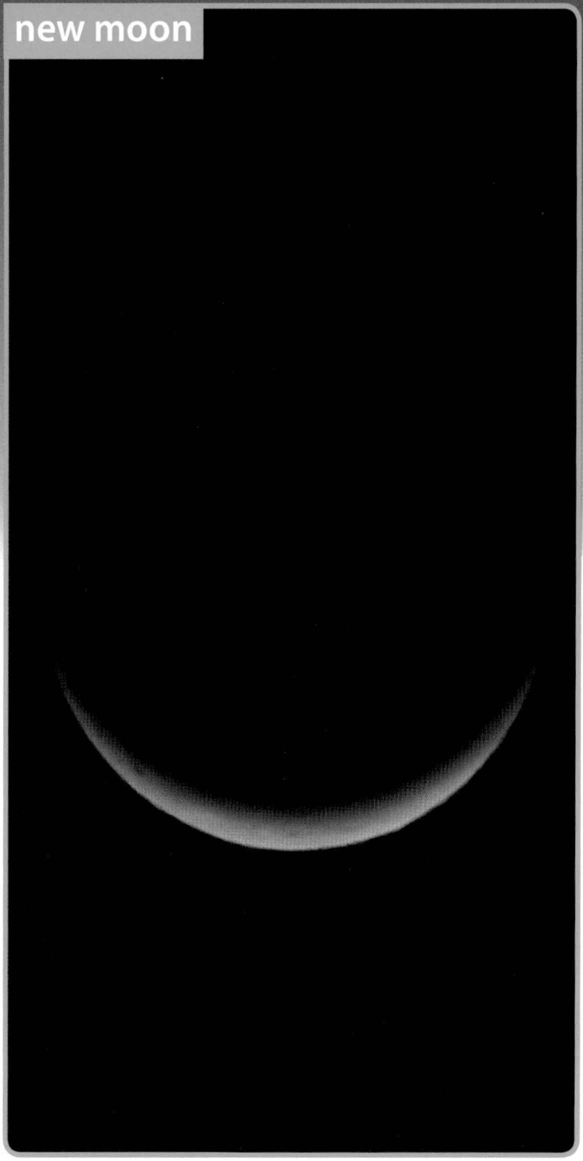

This happens twice. It happens when the moon is full. And it happens when it is just a tiny slice in the sky, a "new moon." At both times, the range is the biggest.

Tide Times

Mon.	Tues.	Wed.	Thurs.	Fri.
9:00	9:50	10:40	11:30	12:20

50 minutes 50 minutes 50 minutes 50 minutes

To check your clock by something, use the tides. Check the times of high and low tides one day. They will happen about 50 minutes later the next day. Check your clock! It should not be too far off! ❖

Endings -er, -est

Read these words.

kid	balloon	bigger	bike	dog
happier	highest	kite	lowest	slimmest

Find the words with **–er** and **–est** endings.
Use letters to build them.

s l i m m e s t

Talk Together

People have fun at the beach when it's low tide! Choose words from the box above to tell your partner about two things you see side by side.

Animal Size Quiz

Do you like to watch shows about animals? See how well you know them. Work with a partner to rank the animals on these pages by size. Talk about it for a while. Begin with the tiniest. Which is a little bigger? A little bigger still? Keep going up to the biggest.

Then ask yourselves: Which animal is oldest? (It lived long, long ago.) Which animal is the hugest and longest living thing by far? (Here's a clue: It's all wet!) Check the answers on the next page. Did you do better than you thought?

1	2	3	4	5	6	7	8	9
Tiniest								**Largest**

blue jay

blue whale

hippo

gray kangaroo

snow goose

saber-toothed tiger

Answer: 1. ladybug 2. blue jay 3. snow goose 4. raccoon 5. gray kangaroo 6. saber-toothed tiger 7. moose 8. hippo 9. blue whale. The oldest animal is the saber-toothed tiger. The hugest and longest is the blue whale.

Acknowledgments
Grateful acknowledgment is given to the authors, artists, photographers, museums, publishers, and agents for permission to reprint copyrighted material. Every effort has been made to secure the appropriate permission. If any omissions have been made or if corrections are required, please contact the Publisher.

Photographic Credits
CVR Panorama Stock RF/Photolibrary. **2** (bcr) DigitalStock/Corbis. (bl) Tony Freeman/PhotoEdit. (br) Glenda M. Powers/Shutterstock. (cl, tr) Eyewire. (tcr) Andrew Buckin/Shutterstock. (tl) Benne Ochs/Getty Images. **3** (b) Liz Garza Williams/Hampton-Brown/National Geographic School Publishing. (cl) Ingram Publishing/Superstock. (cr) Antiques & Collectables/Alamy Images. (l) Hywit Dimyadi/ Shutterstock. (r) C Squared Studios/Photodisc/Getty Images. **4** Siri Stafford/Getty Images. **5** bambooSIL/Photolibrary. **6** (l) gary718/Shutterstock. (r) Sladjana Lukic/iStockphoto. **8** (l) Hans Lang/imagebroker/Alamy Images. (r) Rolf Nussbaumer/Alamy Images. **9** (l) Michael Durham/ Minden Pictures/National Geographic Image Collection. (r) Ferrero Labat/Ardea/Animals Animals. **10** (l) Corel. (r) Thorsten Milse/Mauritius/Photolibrary. **11** (l) Arco Images GmbH/Alamy Images. (r) Thomas Kitchin & Victoria Hurst/First Light/Alamy Images. **12** (l) PhotoDisc/Getty Images. (r) Flying Colours Ltd/Getty Images. **13** (l) Paul Bradbury/Getty Images. (r) Creatas/Jupiterimages. **14** (b, cb, ct) Angelo Cavalli/Digital Vision/Getty Images. (bg) America/Alamy Images. **15** Liz Garza Williams/Hampton-Brown/National Geographic School Publishing. **16** (b) Paul Gapper/Alamy Images. (cl) JingAiping/Shutterstock. (cr) JingAiping/Shutterstock. (t) Vladimirs Koskins/Shutterstock. cc JingAiping/Shutterstock. **17** (b) Liz Garza Williams/Hampton-Brown/National Geographic School Publishing. (t) Kevin Ebi/Alamy Images. **18** NASA Goddard Space Flight Center Image by Reto Stöckli (land surface, shallow water, clouds). Enhancements by Robert Simmon (ocean color, compositing, 3D globes, animation). Data and technical support: MODIS Land Group; MODIS Science Data Support Team; MODIS Atmosphere Group; MODIS Ocean Group Additional data: USGS EROS Data Center (topography); USGS Terrestrial Remote Sensing Flagstaff Field Center (Antarctica); Defense Meteorological Satellite Program (city lights). **20-21** Soren Hald/cultura/Corbis. **23** Ocean Image Photography/Shutterstock. **25** (l, r) Andrew J. Martinez/Photo Researchers, Inc. **27** (l, r) Eyewire. **28** Tony Freeman/PhotoEdit. **29** Liz Garza Williams/Hampton-Brown/National Geographic School Publishing. **3** Jeremy Hoare /LifeFile/PhotoDisc/Getty Images. **30** (b) AlaskaStock. (tl) PureStock/ SuperStock. (tr) John Foxx Images/Imagestate. **31** (bl) Jemini Joseph/Shutterstock. (br) Corbis RF/ Alamy Images. (cl) DigitalStock/Corbis. (cr) Juniors Bildarchiv/Alamy Images. (tl) James Pierce/ Shutterstock. (tr) Hiroya Minakuchi/Minden Pictures/National Geographic Image Collection.

Illustrator Credits
4, **6**, **7**, **22**, **24**, **26** Dartmouth Publishing; **15**, **29** Anne Wilson

National Geographic School Publishing
Hampton-Brown
www.NGSP.com

Printed in the USA.
Quad Graphics, Leominster, MA

ISBN: 978-0-7362-8074-7

17 18 19
10 9 8 7 6 5